To Simon and Jonah
—E.A.K.

First Paper-Over-Board Edition, September 2020
First Hardcover Edition, September 2014
10 9 8 7 6 5 4 3 2 1 • FAC-029191-20248
Printed in Malaysia
Library of Congress Cataloging-in-Publication Control
Number for Hardcover Edition: 2013046370
ISBN 978-1-368-04175-1
Reinforced binding

Visit www.DisneyBooks.com

SIMON AND THE BEAR
a Hanukkah Tale

written by Eric A. Kimmel
illustrated by Matthew Trueman

DISNEY • Hyperion
Los Angeles • New York

When Simon set out for America, he promised his mother and brothers and sisters that he would work hard and save money. As soon as he could, he would send tickets for all of them.

Simon's mother lovingly packed his knapsack for the journey. She put in hard-boiled eggs, salt herring, and two loaves of black bread, heavy as stones. Because Hanukkah was coming, she added something extra.

"I've packed a little menorah, a box of candles, matches, a dreidel, and plenty of latkes," she said, holding back her tears. "Wherever you are, Simon, don't forget to celebrate Hanukkah and its miracles. Who knows? You may need a miracle on your long journey."

Simon took the train to the seaport. There he managed to get the very last ticket for a ship bound for America. His bunk was in the hold, with three hundred other people packed together like herring in a barrel. When the ship sailed, the barrel began to roll.

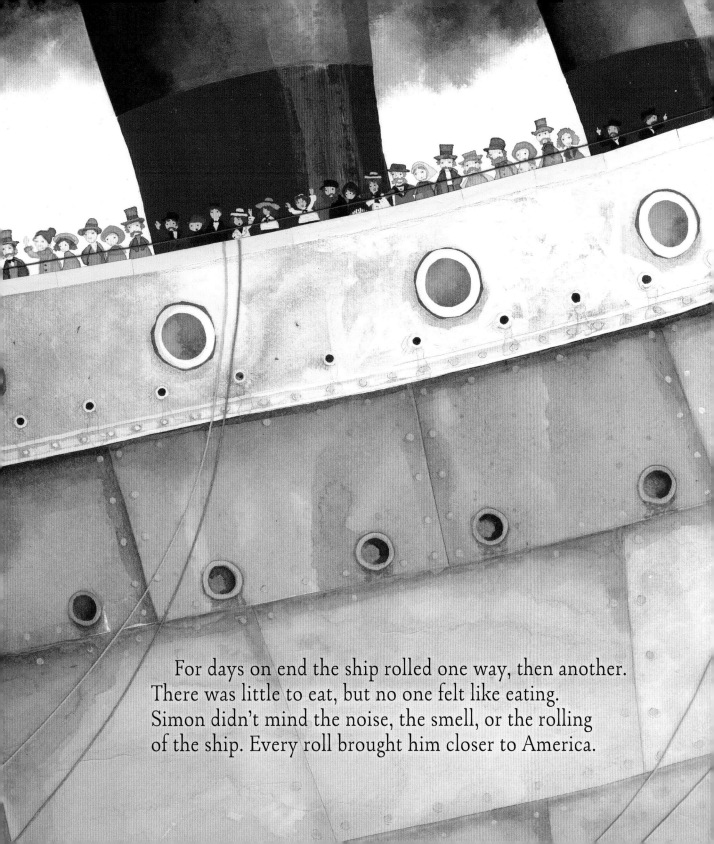

For days on end the ship rolled one way, then another.
There was little to eat, but no one felt like eating.
Simon didn't mind the noise, the smell, or the rolling
of the ship. Every roll brought him closer to America.

One night Simon felt the ship lurch. He heard
sirens and people yelling, "Everyone on deck!"

Simon grabbed his knapsack and ran on deck
with the others. A gigantic wall of ice loomed out
of the sea. Its surface sparkled like diamonds in
the moonlight.

"An iceberg!" Simon heard the sailors shouting.
The ship had struck this floating ice mountain.
Now it was sinking.

Simon stayed on deck, helping people into
the lifeboats until only one boat remained.
Simon climbed in. The sailors began lowering away.

"Don't go! Wait for me!" shouted a man in a fur
coat as he ran across the deck.

"No room!" the sailors shouted at him. "The boat
is full. We'll sink if we take one more person."

The man's face fell. He tossed his watch to Simon. "If you get to New York, give this watch to my little boy. My name is on the back. Tell him Daddy loved him."

The watch felt heavy in Simon's hand. This isn't right, he thought. That little boy will grow up without his father. I know what that feels like.

"Wait!" he called to the sailors. Simon climbed out of the lifeboat. He returned the watch. "Get in, mister. Your boy needs you more than he needs a watch. I'll stay here."

"You're very brave," the man said as he got into the boat. "I'll never forget you."

Simon stood alone on the deck as the lifeboat rowed away. The sinking ship groaned, and its bow lifted into the air. Simon grabbed his knapsack and leaped from the rail just before the ship slipped below the dark water.

Simon landed on the iceberg. He looked up at the moon and said, "Now I am truly alone. I will die here."

He thought sadly about his mother. Then he recalled her parting words. He straightened. "Tonight is the first night of Hanukkah, a time of hope. I won't give up. I'll even light a candle. Who knows? A miracle may happen for me, just as one happened for the Maccabees long ago."

Simon took out his menorah. He said the blessings
and lit the shamash and the first candle. Then he spun his dreidel.
"Gimel is the winning letter," Simon murmured as he watched
the dreidel spin. "But I don't need Gimel. I need Nun. It stands
for *Nes*—Miracle. Come on, dreidel! Give me Nun! Give me a miracle!"

Simon spun his dreidel again and again.
At last it fell on the letter Nun. By then,
the candles had burned out.

In the darkness, Simon heard a splash nearby. Then he
made out a ghostly shape swimming toward him.
It pulled itself onto the iceberg and shook all over.

Simon found himself staring into
the face of an enormous white bear.

The dreidel dropped from his hand. The bear sniffed at it. Then she sniffed Simon's knapsack.

"Are you hungry, bear?" Simon said brightly, trying not to show his fear. Slowly and carefully, he opened his pack. "Have I got a treat for you!" he said. He handed a latke to the bear, who gobbled it down.

"Delicious, isn't it? Have some more," Simon cooed. "Better to eat latkes than to eat me!"

After two more latkes the bear was still hungry, so Simon gave her his black bread and herring. She didn't care for the hard-boiled eggs. Simon ate those himself. Then the bear lay down on the ice and went to sleep.

A cold wind blew across the ocean, and Simon shivered.
"I wonder if the bear will let me get close to her, out of the wind."

He crept over to the bear and snuggled against her fur.
The bear growled in her sleep. She stretched her paw over Simon
as if he were one of her cubs. Simon closed his eyes. He slept
safe and warm that night.

When Simon awoke the next morning, the bear was gone.
He felt lonelier than ever. "Will she come back?" he wondered.
For what seemed like hours he stared out at the empty horizon.

Then he saw something white
bobbing on the waves. It was the bear,
swimming toward him!

The bear climbed back on the ice. Simon saw that she had a fish in her mouth. She skinned it with her teeth, and then, to his surprise, she bit it in two and gave him half.

Simon cut it up with his pocketknife and tried a piece. "Not bad!" he told the bear. "A little salty. Like lox." He and the bear ate the fish together. The bear went fishing again, and that night, when Simon lit the second Hanukkah candle, his stomach was full.

Over the next few days the bear swam off in the morning to fish and returned in the afternoon with her catch. Every night Simon lit one more candle in the menorah. He shared his latkes and entertained the bear with Hanukkah songs and stories. Then they curled up together to go to sleep.

"This is truly a miracle. And not the only one," Simon said to himself. He counted the miracles on his fingers. He'd gotten the last ticket. He'd found a place in the lifeboat. He'd saved a man's life. He'd jumped on the iceberg, not in the ocean. The bear didn't eat him. She brought him food. She kept him warm.

Seven miracles! Simon looked out across the sea. "It will take another miracle for me to be rescued. Is one more too much to ask for?"

The last night of Hanukkah arrived. Simon lit the candles. As they burned out one by one, leaving him in utter darkness, he thought, I have no more candles, no more matches. Tonight we ate the last latke. My knapsack is empty. No bread, no eggs, no herring. Maybe the bear will swim away tomorrow. Then no fish. I will surely die of cold and hunger.

Simon shivered as the moon rose over the cold sea. "I have run out of miracles," he said.

Suddenly the bear stood up on her hind legs. She sniffed the air. Dropping down, she jumped into the ocean and swam away. "Bear! Where are you going? Don't leave me!" Simon called after her.

Immediately, he heard other voices. "Ahoy! You on the ice! Stay where you are! We've come to rescue you."

A passing ship had seen the light of his Hanukkah candles and sent a boat to investigate. Simon had his eighth miracle. He was saved!

The ship brought Simon to New York. His story appeared in all the newspapers. Simon became a celebrity. The mayor gave him the key to the city. And the mayor was . . . the man in the fur coat!

"You saved my life," the mayor told Simon. "What can I do for you?"

"Find me a job, so I can bring my family to America," Simon asked.

"I will buy their tickets today. First class," the mayor promised. "As for a job, I have one I think you'll enjoy."

BOY

Simon Kemelhaar, the been found alive. A wire how the boy was found on how he managed to survive Mayor William J. Gayno come Mr. Kemelhaar at his ment of Immigration has agre heroic lad. "That boy saved m at an interview this mo him do

HERO FOUND ALIVE

by Kerry Himmel

g Russian immigrant who saved New York City's mayor, has
essage received hours ago from the U.S.S. Corvallis describes
ting iceberg. He is reported to be in good health. It is unclear
re than a week after the tragic sinking of the H.M.S. Atlantic
ead an official delegation of New York's civic le
ed arrival on Ellis Island three d
waive all entranc

Just as the Hanukkah menorah has one extra candle, the shamash, so too did Simon receive one extra miracle. The mayor found him the perfect job— as Polar Bear Keeper at the Central Park Zoo!

"Which goes to show that miracles aren't just for the Maccabees," Simon told his friends and family every year at Hanukkah time. "They can happen to anyone, anywhere, even in the darkest of times. You just have to believe."

Hanukkah, the Jewish Festival of Lights, commemorates a victory over the occupying Greek forces in 164 B.C.E. Jerusalem was liberated and worship at the Temple restored. According to legend, there was only enough sacred oil to light the menorah, the seven-branched golden candlestick, for one day. Yet it burned for eight, until more oil could be brought to the city.

Since then, Hanukkah has been celebrated with light and oil. The Hanukkah Lamp, called a menorah or hanukiyyah, is lit every night for eight days. Traditional Hanukkah foods include potato pancakes, or latkes, which are fried in oil. The dreidel, a four-sided top, bears the letters Nun, Gimel, Hay, and Shin. These stand for the Hebrew phrase *Nes Gadol Haya Sham—A Great Miracle Happened There.*